I'm Special!

Acknowledgments

Executive Editor: Diane Sharpe
Supervising Editor: Stephanie Muller
Design Manager: Sharon Golden
Page Design: Simon Balley Design Associates
Photography: Greg Evans: page 9; Chris Fairclough: page 17; Alex Ramsay: page 19; Tony Stone: cover (top left), pages 7, 11, 13, 15, 21; ZEFA: cover (middle left, right), pages 5, 23, 25, 27.

Library of Congress Cataloging-in-Publication Data

Humphrey, Paul, 1952-
    I'm special! / Paul Humphrey; illustrated by Nick Ward.
      p.   cm. — (Read all about it)
    Summary: Drawings, photographs, and brief captions depict children telling what is special about themselves and their friends and relatives.
    ISBN 0-8114-5725-7 Hardcover
    ISBN 0-8114-3739-6 Softcover
    [1. Individuality — Fiction.]   I. Ward, Nick, ill.   II. Title.   III. Series: Read all about it (Austin, Tex.)
PZ7.H8973Im 1995
[E]—dc20

94-28579
CIP
AC

1 2 3 4 5 6 7 8 9 0 PO 00 99 98 97 96 95 94

I'm Special!

Paul Humphrey

Illustrated by
Nick Ward

STECK-VAUGHN
COMPANY
ELEMENTARY • SECONDARY • ADULT • LIBRARY

I'm special!

4

No one else is just like me.

6

I can score a goal in soccer.

8

I can paint beautiful pictures.

9

I can play music on my violin.

11

I can read books.

I can help in the kitchen.

15

I can learn new things.

I can swim from one end of
the pool to the other end.

20

We play together.

22

He plays games with me.

24

She makes me smile when
I'm sad.

25

26

They read many stories to us.

We can all do something
that makes us special.

All of these people are special.
Do you remember why?

Index